THE PINK PARROT

written and illustrated by

Gill McBarnet

Ruwanga  Trading

Also published by Ruwanga Trading:
The Whale Who Wanted to be Small
The Wonderful Journey

First published 1986 by
Ruwanga Trading
P.O. Box 1027
Puunene
Hawaii 96784

Printed and bound in Hong Kong
under direction of:
Mandarin Offset Marketing (H.K.) Ltd.

ISBN 0-9615102-1-8

For Mom and Dad

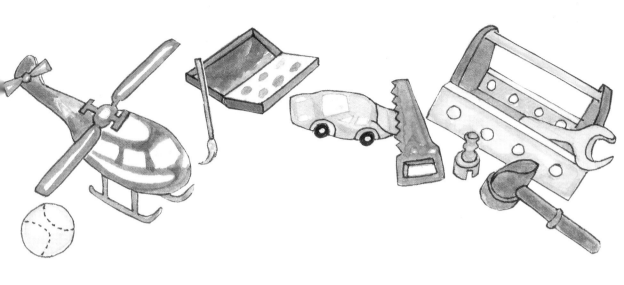

Of all Eddie's favorite toys, playdough is what he
liked to play with best.
One day, Eddie made a big ball of playdough. It was
plump and pink and he started to squash it with his
hands. As he pinched and pulled at the pink ball, it
seemed to come to life.
He made a fierce dinosaur
        and then a snake.
The snake became an octopus with many legs
        and then the octopus got squashed and twisted
        and patted and pulled into...

...a parrot!

The pink parrot had big strong wings,
long tail feathers and a perky head that was tipped
mischievously to one side.
"Time for your afternoon nap, Eddie" called his Mum.
"Hey, Mum. My parrot winked at me!" shouted Eddie.
"Did he indeed?" replied his Mum. "Perhaps your
parrot would like a nap too. Why not put him next to
you while you sleep?"
Eddie played with his parrot for a bit. Then he put the
parrot carefully beside him before settling
down to sleep.

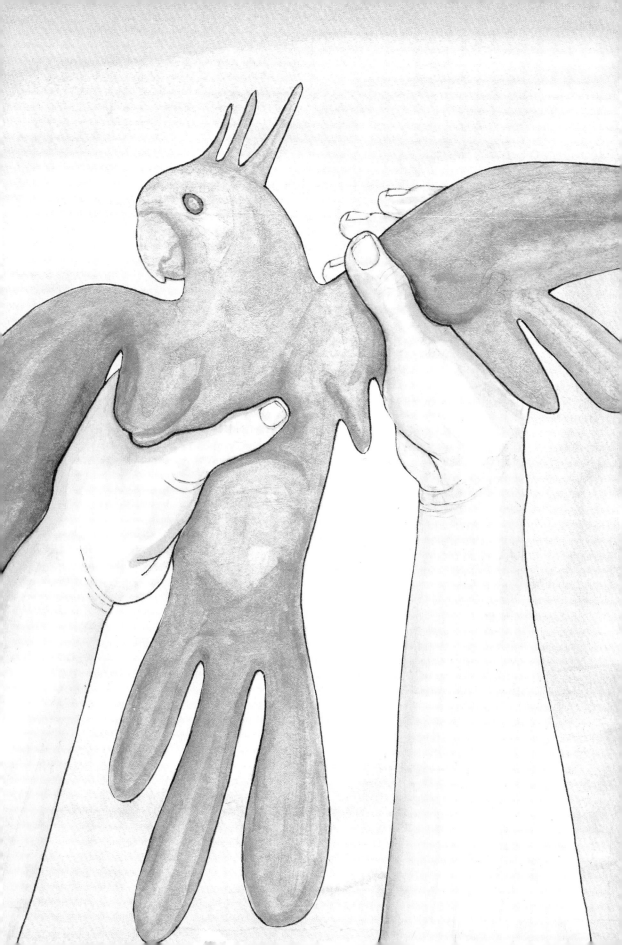

"What was, that?" Eddie woke up with a start when he heard something move alongside him.

"Don't be afraid. It's only me" came the soft reply.

"Who is *me*?" asked Eddie sleepily.

"Why, I'm the pink parrot you made today. Don't you remember?"

There was a flutter of wings and a pink bird flew over to the window. Sure enough, there was his parrot perched on the window ledge, stretching her wings and preening herself in the sunshine.

"Since you have given me the gift of life, I would like to give you a gift, Eddie. You can wish for anything you like, and I will make your wish come true."
"Anything?" asked Eddie.
"Yes, anything you like" replied the parrot. "But don't take too long thinking about it because when the sun sets in the evening sky, I will become playdough again."
"I'd love to go to faraway lands" Eddie eagerly exclaimed. "Only trouble is, how will I get there?"

"Climb onto my back and I will fly you there" said the parrot.

As she spoke she spread her wings, and Eddie noticed she was growing bigger and bigger until...

...she was just the right size to carry Eddie.

Out of the window they flew, up and up into a clear blue sky. The air felt cool and soft against his cheeks as the parrot flew Eddie further and further away from his house.

They flew over a dry yellow land and a boy waved at them as they passed overhead. A rattlesnake lay coiled in the shadow of a cactus, and a fox trotted quickly through the long yellow grass.

On and on the parrot flew, over vast blue oceans to a land of ice and snow. Icicles hung like diamonds in the pale afternoon sun. A polar bear padded stealthily across the soft white snow, and seals slipped quickly away into the ice blue sea. Some children were fishing, and they stared in amazement as the parrot flew by.

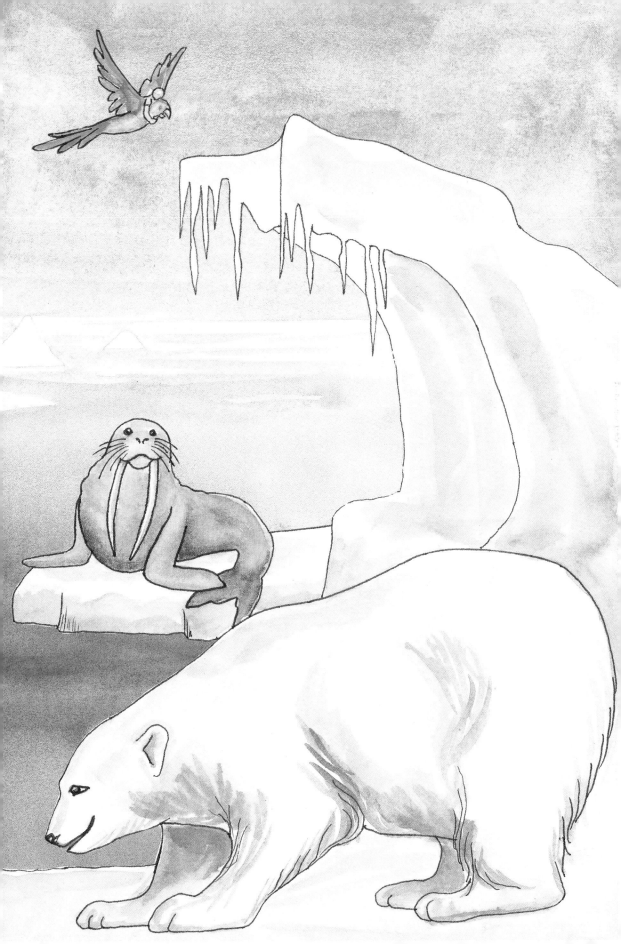

Further and further they flew.
They flew through gentle woodlands where deer
danced in and out of the shadows. There were flowers
of every shape and colour, and rabbits nibbled the
tender young dandelions. Fieldmice and hedgehogs
scurried about, and Eddie noticed a squirrel gathering
acorns. A girl was picking flowers, and she smiled up
at them as they flew overhead.

The parrot took Eddie to places he had never imagined existed. Deserts, where camels plodded slowly through golden sand and lizards basked lazily in the hot hot sun. Children pointed at them and waved as they flew high above. They cast a shadow on the burning sand but soon that, too, was gone.

Then on and on, to wide open plains where Eddie saw many animals that he had never seen before. Monkeys playing in the trees and a lion crouched low in the grass below. Rosy flamingoes on delicate legs, and the haunting cry of a fish eagle echoed behind them as they continued on their way.

They flew far far away to forests frilled with ferns and ringing with the song of many different kinds of birds. A tiger trod quietly by, his eyes flashing like yellow jewels. A young boy watched them as the parrot soared up into the sky again. Higher and higher, leaving the forest far behind them.

Next they flew to a wide, slow river. Water lilies grew near its banks and panda bears rested in the whispering bamboo. Ducks quacked noisily to each other, and cormorants dived deep in searched of fish.

The parrot was getting tired so he came down to rest in a cool, shady tree. Eddie saw koalas munching the leaves of the blue gum tree. Kangaroos bounded gracefully beneath them, and a baby kangaroo peeped curiously at them from his mother's warm pouch.

At last they came to a tropical island in the middle of the ocean. Eddie joyfully wiggled his toes in the soft, warm sand. The blue waves were laced with white foam, and shells lay scattered all over the beach. A turtle lay nearby and dolphins played in the palm fringed bay.

When the sun was low in the sky, the parrot said "Come Eddie we must go now. We have visited many wonderful faraway lands, but I must get you home before the sun sets in the evening sky."

Eddie snuggled against the parrot's soft feathers and in no time he was fast asleep. The sky slowly flooded with the pink and golden light of sunset, as the parrot flew closer and closer to Eddie's house.

There was just a tip of red sun peeping over the treetops, when the parrot flew into Eddie's bedroom. Very gently, so as not to wake him, the parrot carefully lay Eddie down on his bed.

"Hmmm" sighed Eddie dreamily, still clinging to the parrot's neck. The parrot softly nudged Eddie onto his pillow and as he did so, a feather came away in Eddie's hand.

Slowly, and a little stiffly, the parrot fluttered over to
the window. As he settled on the window ledge he
looked back at Eddie, gave a sweet little smile and
then closed his eyes.

Soon he too was asleep.

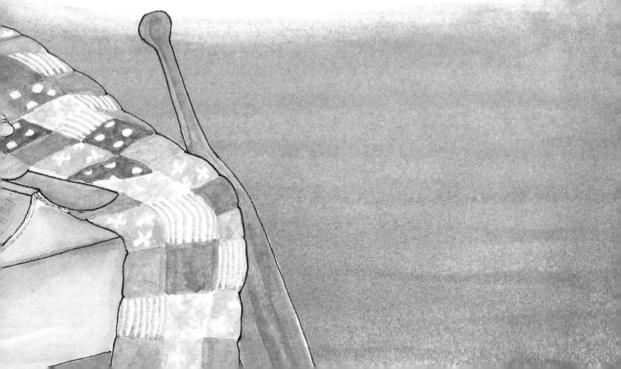

Eddie woke up to hear his Mum calling him for supper.

"Oh Mum, I had such a wonderful time. I visited faraway lands on the back of my parrot!"

"You visited those faraway lands in your dreams, Eddie! You had such a nice long sleep, but come along now or your dinner will get cold" his Mum replied.

"But I tell you I *did*" exclaimed Eddie. "If you don't believe me, ask my pink parrot." As he was speaking, he looked around, but all that remained of his parrot was a big pink ball of playdough.

"Oh no, oh no..." Eddie started to cry. But suddenly he realized that he was holding something soft and silky in his hand.

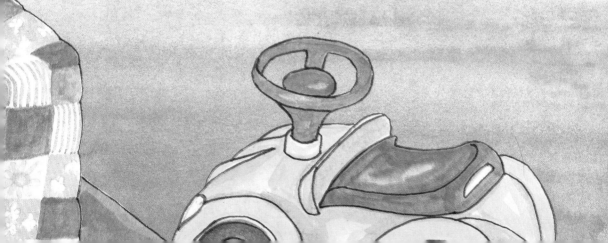

His tears stopped as quickly as they had started when he looked down at his hands. Clutched tightly in his fingers was the most beautiful feather you could possibly imagine, and it seemed to glow like a pink flame.

Eddie smiled a secret smile as he stroked the pink feather. His dream to visit faraway lands had come true, and he would always remember his friend the pink parrot.

Faraway Lands

 Dry Yellow Lands

 Ice and Snow

 Gentle Woodlands

 Desert

 Wide Open Plains

 Forests

 Whispering Bamboo

 Blue Gum Trees

 Tropical Island